HOW DARE YOU?

Jodi Adler

HOW DARE YOU?

Helpful Hints for Staying Sane in an Insane World

Ginger Jam Media
Los Angeles, California

auntiejodi.com

ISBN: 978-0-9907276-0-6

Book design by Timothy Griggs

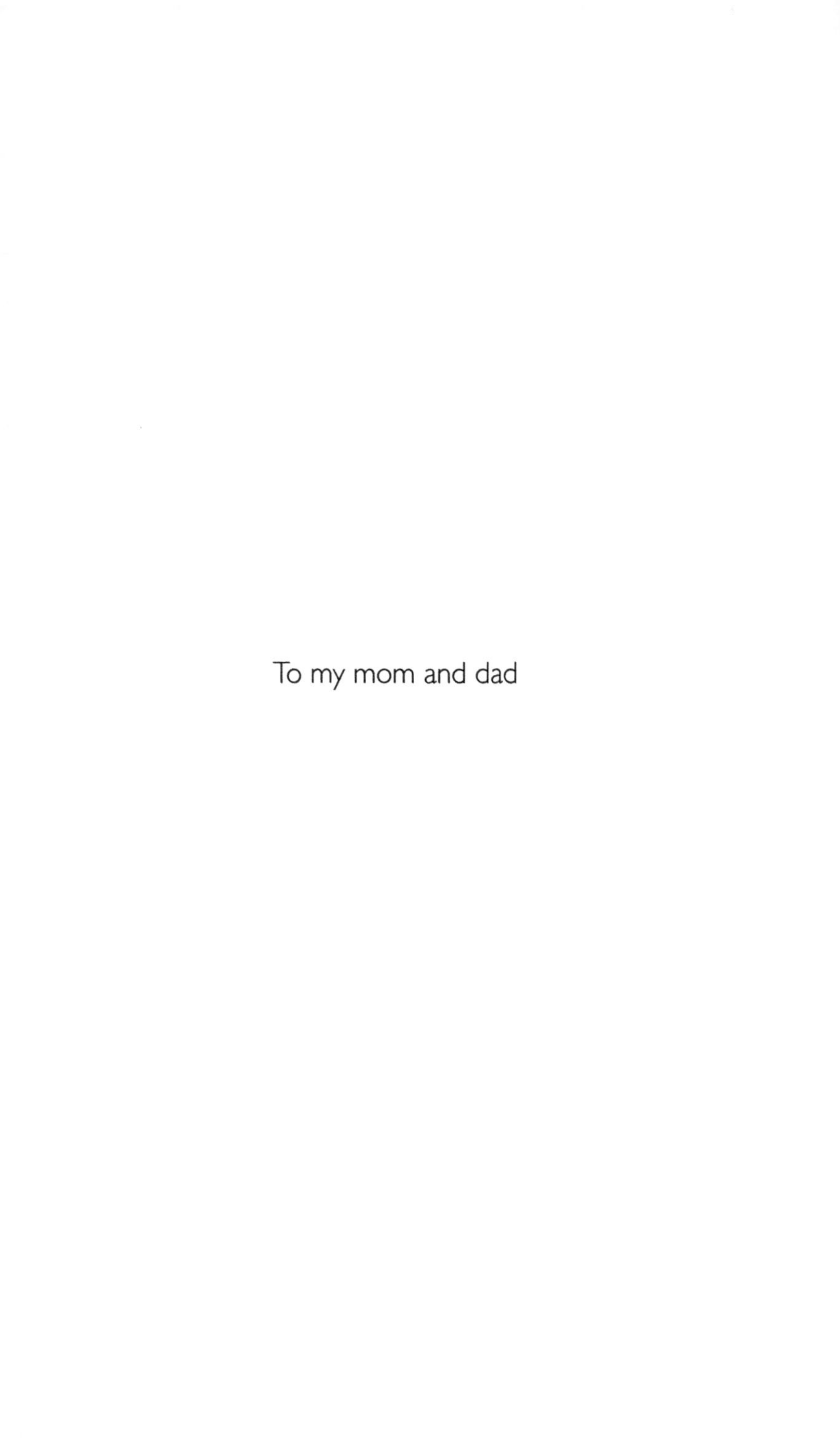

To my mom and dad

Here's a Helpful Hint:
Join Auntie online and keep your etiquette skills sharp.

auntiejodi.com

Table of Contents

Introduction

Time and time again Auntie Jodi has found herself upset and beset by the crass, rude, walk-all-over-you crowd who seem to be running our world right now. Whenever she'd stand up for herself, defending her sweet soul against the pushy, bossy, boorish types who seem to be winning, not only would she feel bad, often she'd think that perhaps she'd not said enough—perhaps the rude ones need to be put in their place—politely, of course, but with a bit of sarcasm and sass that says, "do that again and you'll be sorry." And so with that in mind, Auntie Jodi's Helpful Hints was born.

Auntie Jodi did not start out in life with a readily available response to all the nasty and noisy—believe it or not, little Jodi was often the shyest girl in the room. It probably started in kindergarten—her teacher did not know what to do with the oh-so-quiet Jodi—but her smart and sassy mother set that teacher straight by telling her, "There's nothing wrong with Jodi, she's just polite." Yes, Auntie Jodi does have the best mom on the planet—and at that moment, the path was cleared for Auntie's calling in life.

It wasn't always easy standing up to the bullies—in first grade, Auntie had to take down two nasty fifth graders who were taunting her in the girls' bathroom. Never had a "punch and run" felt so good. Yes, little Jodi was called into the principal's office (her one and only time) and while she was told to never punch anyone again (Auntie's mostly keep that promise)—the two older bullies were severely admonished and sent to another school. Jodi learned then and there that (politely) standing up for oneself was always the right thing to do.

That moment in the principal's office led her teacher to promote Jodi as the protector of all the weak and bullied kids in the class—a job that no six-year-old ever took more seriously—this, in the days before any large-scale anti-bullying campaign ever existed. Now that Auntie is a few decades out of first grade, her anti-bullying campaigning continues—in a slightly different form.

Bullying is indeed, a word that is misused these days—but it is a growing phenomenon—so how do we stop these nasty souls from ruining our day? If possible, try to ignore them. If not, use Auntie Jodi's Helpful Hints to politely even the score. When Auntie was a broadcast journalist, one of her bosses was certifiably crazy (okay maybe more than one). And what did Auntie always do in response? Something she suggests you do: Use your smarts and humor—turn those dear souls around, send them back on their nasty path and get back on your road to happiness. Why not learn Morse Code and tap out a four-letter word on your desk every time they enter the room? Yes, it's passive aggressive. Yes, they probably won't know what you're doing. And yes, you will laugh and feel a million times better.

So get busy reading—select a few hints, make them your own, and use them as the need arises. And if you have any questions for Auntie Jodi—just send her a note—who knows, you may find your predicament included (with a personalized Helpful Hint) in the next edition of Auntie Jodi's Helpful Hints.

Here's a hint—you don't have to read this book in any particular order—just thumb through and begin.

Jodi Adler

Chapter 1

Friends & Family

Sometimes, the most difficult people we have to deal with are those who fall into the "Friends and Family" category. Yes, we can certainly disown family members (Auntie has had to do this with a select few). And yes, we can unfriend those who are hopeless and crass.

But what if, a Helpful Hint or word to the wise helps to corral those friends and family members, making interactions a breeze? That, my darlings is what this chapter is all about—they are your friends for a reason, right? Perhaps a hint or two would help...so here are a few of Auntie's favorites...

Auntie Jodi does not believe in ***"frenemies."*** You are either my friend or you are not my friend. She **ardently** believes that she does not belong in the same atelier as those **frenemy** people. Let's just call those loathsome creatures manipulative **losers**, and be done with **them**.

Hate small talk? Bring up **politics**, and as soon as you find two people with differing **opinions**, bring them **together**. If they refuse to hold hands while singing ***"We Are the World,"*** offer to moderate a debate between them. Give them ten minutes to prep. This works really well if relatives are **involved**.

This works **exceptionally** well if there is an ***"Upstairs-Downstairs"*** or ***"Downton Abbey"*** situation in the hosts' home. Instead of **mingling**, find a way into the kitchen, and offer to help **the help.** Don't talk, just listen—chances are you will learn oodles about your hosts. This newfound **information** will help you with small talk/**blackmail** in the future.

It is always fun to get an **unexpected gift**—and a thoughtful, anonymous present to someone who actually needs something can be **kind** and caring. Know someone full of hot air? Tastefully wrap up a bottle of **Beano** and send it overnight express. **Remember**, it is immature to always need recognition for good deeds, so do not worry about getting a **thank-you** note.

Feel like giving that fake **compliment-giver** a smack in her fake-talking mouth? **Remember** to always be gracious, say ***"thank you,"*** and reciprocate as soon as possible. Why not have a sincere retort at the ready? How about, ***"You look ever so much better since your surgery."***

Getting **wedding**, shower or coming of age party **invitations** from people you haven't seen in **years**? Just because you have a reputation as a great **gift-giver**, do not get cynical about the reason for this reconnection. Attend, and make a donation to a controversial **non-PC** cause dear to your heart—the greater the **controversy**, the greater your chance of not having to worry about another gift-begging **invite**.

Go through your list of **friends** every so often, and reassess that once-so-special **connection**. Is an old pal now living under an **assumed** name? Perhaps it's time to assume that **sharing** any information with this dear one needs to halted. **Off-kilter** funny buddy now forgetting to take his meds? It's time to say, ***"Kiss bye-bye."*** Keep your sanity by tossing away your old save-a-soul self. The **soul** you now save might just be your own.

Find yourself trying to **connect** the dots, only to end up with false positives, stale gossip, and bits of misinformation about everything? **Auntie** finds it increasingly amusing that people jump to **outrageous** conclusions about all sorts of things simply because of the way someone looks, their **political** affiliation, or their zip code. Leave the real sleuthing to the nation's spooks—so you are free to go back to reading the latest romance or **thriller**, while chatting about matters of greater importance—such as Grace's bad hair color or boob job.

Here's a way to subtly **show off** your new tattoo. Oh wait, there is no way to be subtle with a new **tatt...** Just strategically shred a t-shirt so it **highlights** your inky creation. While at the gym, you won't have to wait long as your friends gaze/gawk/gander at the **brilliance** of your ink and your obvious intellectual **prowess**.

Know someone who takes more than the **proverbial** foot when nary an inch is offered? With this sort, it is best to rein in all offers at all times. To counter their **misuse** and manipulation of your thoughtfulness, immediately end all **interaction** with those who fail to appreciate our sincere help and **kind** efforts.

When catching someone in a **lie**, the **issue** is not necessarily the lie, it is the sure-thing/guaranteed bet that this poor **soul** will indeed, lie again. To counteract any such future **problems** with the delusional soul, suggest he or she write down all responses to any query of yours. Do not waste their **creativity**—simply sign them up as a writing partner—making sure your **contract** is the best boilerplate you can find.

Find that some of the people in your inner **circle** have issues correctly citing your bon mots, retorts, and opinions? Keep a pocket-pack of **Q-tips** at the ready, and when handing them out to your **misquoting** companions, suggest they clean that nasty wax out of their **ears**—as you permanently clean, delete, or fire-bomb these folk off of your **contacts** list.

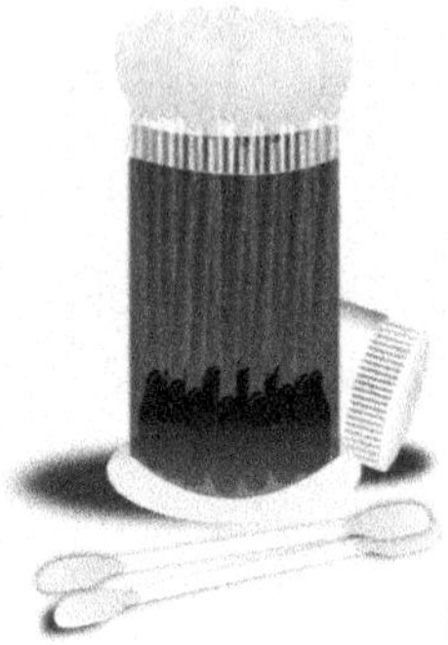

Never let a **grudge** go to waste. The key with grudges is to pretend you have **"moved on,"** while plotting your **revenge**. When you finally get to zing, prank, or kill your victim, no one will ever suspect you are the evil **mastermind**.

Do you have friends with **habitual** tardiness issues? Start keeping track of their **on-time** record, so that you might compare their numbers with your least favorite **airline's** on-time stats. Politely bring this up after their lateness record surpasses the airline's (have charts and documentation at the ready). Then request an upgrade to **First Class**, which in this case, means a downgrade in any future invitations sent to these self-involved, **egocentric**, arrogant folk.

Does every **family** get-together become a real life episode of the game show **Family Feud**? Why not make this year's reunion pay off—for at least one branch of your family tree. Evenly divide the group, and then go around the **table**, asking prepared questions of all the attendees. Turn up the fun by providing everyone with a noisemaker/buzzer so that no whispering or **cheating** can occur without being called out. Provide a cash **payout**—a small annuity works best—to the winning side. Assign the **losers** to KP duty.

When **Auntie** was growing up, we all learned how to be **gracious** winners and losers, though it seems that this sort of instruction has skipped a **generation**—or two. Some dear dolts must now be **taught** what it means to be a gracious winner or to—**gasp**—lose at a competitive event. This means that you must not **boast**, gloat, or rub your foe's nose in their **loss**—doing such a thing makes you the ultimate loser. Auntie believes that **friendship** is a greater gift than any passing victory.

Darling, when you talk to Ms. Friend about **Auntie** or anyone else, you put Ms. Friend into a very precarious position . . . it's called **gossip**, or lashon hara—and yes, my sweet, it is a sin. Make sure you have your **facts** straight—in every aspect of your life—before you talk about someone. (Unless of course you are a **writer** of fiction. Then write it all down, and give Auntie a formal **dedication**, kudos, or credit as your muse—with the all-important contracted residual stream in perpetuity.)

When relaying **stories** to a friend, dinner companion, or large crowd, remember to insert the phrase ***"spoiler alert"*** every so often. Not only does it draw in the multitasker or technology **geek**, it also gives your story an extra bit of **cachet**—which will cause your tale to be repeated just often enough for you to become an internet **legend**.

Have you recently discovered a small group of **evil**, envious leeches has snuck into your world? If you were not so fabulously funny, **gorgeous**, smart, witty, wealthy, polite, successful, endearingly nice, charitable, and **sexy** . . . those envious people would have nothing to talk about. Excise the poor **souls** from your life by hiring them as assistants, sending them off on some **wild** errands . . . and then taking notes for your next best-seller as they attempt to get some **real work** done.

When dealing with **children**, be they yours or others', you must include the slow **head** turn/stare/look of **disdain** in your repertoire of reactions. If this does not immediately work, I suggest immediately **lacing** the parent's and child's food/milk/juice with an 80-proof **spirit**.

Can't get enough of holidays like International **Coffee** Day, **Sweetest** Day, or National Mustard Day? Create your own special day. Refrain from going to work, and petition the local legislature to **acknowledge** your specialness. Let's call tomorrow National **Sleeping** It Off Day, next Monday International **Estheticians'** Day . . . and don't forget every dance lover's favorite, **Cha Cha** Thursday (I think that'll be in March).

Those darling little **children** of yours down with the **flu**? Simply go on an impromptu vacay with your **hubby** . . . by the time you come back, the kiddies will be **healthy** as can be.

Clueless cad or **greedy** gal issue invites to his/her ***"no host"*** birthday party at a local hot-spot? Be careful if you should decide to attend this **soiree**. Auntie always errs on the side of generosity, but more often than not, we generous **attendees** end up footing more than our fair **share** of the tacky host's and cheap guests' bill. Bring a limited amount of greenbacks, be generous when tipping the **help**, but do not allow yourself to be guilt-tripped into **paying** for the cheapskates in our midst. In fact, this just might be the only time to **discreetly** ask for separate checks.

Auntie Jodi knows you are proud of yourself, but sometimes, just **sometimes** . . . you may want to rethink that chest **thumping**. It sounds as if you're bragging. Perhaps it might be better to just let us accidentally find out how **wonderful** you are. The art of being subtle is so sorely **missed** these days.

Is a dear one hinting for a bit of **flattery** about a new item of clothing, haircut, or accessory that is simply **hideous** or beyond **ugly**? Respond to that needy plea with the phrase, ***"That's so you!"*** Voilà—the dear one's Neanderthal tastes are not called into question. For fun, you might take a photo so the look can be submitted to a **fashion** disaster/makeover columnist.

Spy someone's **designer** label hanging out the back of their collar? Your response on this one depends on your **relationship** with the label dangler. Do you like him or her? **Discreetly** position yourself close enough to whisper a warning, and possibly help with the tuck-in. Not a fan? Ignore the dangling label; it's probably a **knock-off** jacket anyway.

Do not **hate**; it makes you ugly. Instead, think about plotting **revenge**. This course of action not only takes a wonderful **imagination**, and increases your circle of friends, but it also provides years of happiness—which of course, makes you look ages **younger**.

Too many **people** with too many problems trying to suck some of your **happy** spirit away? Turn on your inner ***"who cares?"*** switch, and readjust your personal settings. Whenever someone **overshares** yet another tidbit from the inner workings of his or her life, stare . . . then smile, and reset. Keep repeating this mantra: ***"Who cares. Go away."*** Uttering the phrase aloud helps speed up the ***"go away"*** part of the process, of course.

Planning a **party**, and trying to take the fashionably late friends' habits into account? Counter their **tardiness** by sending out invitations with staggered start times. Take bets with the **help** about who will actually show up before the **flambé** goes cold.

Know someone who always needs to have the last **word**? Shut down this neurotic know-it-all with sing-song phrases such as, ***"told ya so,"*** or the always popular tiff-ender, ***"are not, are too."*** If this still does not work, then stick out your tongue and say ***"Nah nah nah NAH nah."***

Overwhelmed/piqued/dismayed by **calls** and messages from people you never met or **never** want to chat with again? Devise a personal ***"do not call list,"*** using criteria such as needy, **soul-sucking**, or not able to understand your humor, and **voila**—you earn back hours, if not days, of freedom from their phone **tyranny**. Now go bless the genius who invented caller ID.

Feeling **sad**, old, or in need of a facelift because of an upcoming birthday/anniversary/renegotiation meeting? Use the ignorance of **teenagers** to your advantage, and ask a few to **guess** your age. Most of their responses will top out at 35 (yes, we know that they naively think **mid-thirties** is old). Nothing feels as good as being told you look years younger than you really are. Just this once, do not **consider** the source.

Surrounded by **petty** nitpickers? The next time one of them dares to point out an **endearing** minor flaw, explain that your life is a **macro** project, and those micro issues are for micro-thinkers. Before smiling and gracefully **exiting**, mention your efforts in helping to increase the money supply, and **note** that scarce resources—like your time—must always be properly **allocated**.

Auntie Jodi wants to remind you of the power of the phrase, ***"I don't know."*** Not only does using it stop a **modern-day** inquisition, it allows you to continue with your tea/**coffee**/

vodka-tasting party duties. Also helpful: ***"I do not have a clue,"*** and ***"I plead the fifth."*** It is always best if any of these phases is uttered with absolute solemn sincerity.

Absent-minded friend constantly misplacing her **glasses**, keys, bracelet or rings while visiting? Make the hunt for the lost items part of a game of **Hide and Seek**. If you should find the item before your pal, quickly assess its **Antiques Roadshow** auction value before handing it over.

Overbooking, **neurotic**, socialite-poseur pestering you for a luncheon **date**—but only if you **rearrange** your life for her tightly ordered one-hour window of opportunity? Have an iron-clad agenda of your own and wage a one-on-one battle of **schedules**. Always remember to use terms such as life coach, banker, parole officer, or **Pilates** instructor, so the importance of your schedule always trumps those **trifling** conflicts in her petty little schedule.

Are those **anger** management classes failing to ease the ongoing **friction** at home? Learn to properly channel that desire to slap, punch, or **throttle** your dear ones by taking to the stage at a local **comedy** club's open mic night—then watch as your fan base explodes. Be ready to sign with one of the top **agents**, who will find you just the right script—transforming you into the **funniest,** most highly paid, cutting edge comic on the planet.

Find that your phone **calls** are not being returned, your text **messages** are being missed, or you've been dropped, perhaps even **un-friended** by an acquaintance or long-time pal? No need to worry yourself about this ungrateful lout: if anyone leaves your inner **circle** without explanation, they need to look long and hard into a **mirror**. Only a coward leaves a relationship, **soirée**, or government appointment without at least a nod, **handshake**, or filing of a formal complaint.

Is a needy acquaintance continually reminding you that your offhand/spot-on **comments** are being taken—ahem—***"personally"?*** **Auntie** knows that dear one's unresolved family issues always make for some **hideously** tiresome exchanges. Suggest that this over-sensitive soul stop making every matter, from holiday table seating assignments to **best-selling** book reviews and theater **critiques**, a topic of blathering debate. However, if the need for a lethal duel develops—then by all means, sharpen your blade and **plunge** right in.

Auntie wants to remind her dear friends that we may nod and listen to your **tale** of woe the first two, three, or four times. We may even appear to hang on every word, as you retell your story of a personal world gone **mad** . . . but in reality, our responses are simply the result of a good upbringing. Your job, **dear one**, is to look up the meaning of the word ***"discretion."*** Shut down your self-serving urge to tell us your sordid story one more time, especially if we should ever again cross **paths**.

Should you be **distressed** about another driver's actions, make sure your **toddler** has earplugs firmly planted in his sweet little ears before you launch into a **vulgar**, profane, and tired tirade. It is true: one day, when you least expect it, your sweet little toddler will surprise you with his stupendous **four-letter** word-recall skills.

Auntie would like to request that if you have children, you assume the role of **parent** at all times until each child is 18 or of sound mind (that condition may require an **additional** decade). Just because something is cute, trendy, or funny does not make the **behavior** welcome in **restaurants**, or houses of worship—or, for that matter, in any **public** forum.

Auntie would never suggest that anyone hold back from speaking from the **heart**. Despite some oft-cited rules of polite society, being **opinionated** is much preferred to leading a common, fearful, milquetoast life. However, it may sometimes serve to hold back from **stating** your point of view in order to see where some newly made friends, soon to be sworn **enemies**, actually stand.

Are you dealing with a tedious dear one who claims, ***"I never drink alone"?*** Have pity on the poor dear and offer to show her how—while in her company, pour a single **vodka** martini, and sip on it while conversing with her. Not only will you have made your point, you will have survived a chat that might have been deadly dull—had you lacked the foresight to **drink** alone.

1. Does Auntie believe in frienemies?
2. What assignment is given to the losers of a game of holiday Family Feud?
3. When is Cha Cha Thursday?

Chapter II

Relationships

Ahhhh Relationships... if only dealing with an ardent or not-so-ardent love was as easy as pouring a glass of Prosecco. Auntie has had her share of issues in the area of relationships...and the key is to never give up on finding your Prince or Princess.

So as you seek out that wonderful mate for your soul, why not have a bit of fun? That was always Auntie's methodology. Remember—even through the broken heart phase, there will be time to laugh... not only at those losers who don't know what you're worth, but most importantly, at your own sweet self...

If you're trying to **impress**/date/ marry **Auntie** Jodi, using the phrase ***"get with me"*** is not going to help your sales pitch. Really. You cannot possibly be serious. Now go away. **Forever**.

Have you been sneered at for using the phrase, ***"THE wife"*** (or ***"THE hubby"***)? Why not have a giggle at tonight's gathering by substituting a number in place of **"the."** Watch jaws drop when you say, ***"my first wife..."*** This is hugely amusing if you are still on your first **marriage**.

Has someone who is suffering from **Excessive Hugging Syndrome** invaded your space one time too many? Combat those overhuggers/boobsquishers simply by quickly turning your body ninety degrees as the **hugger** lunges toward you. Speedy reflexes and practice will you help perfect this **technique**. If all else fails, remember to quickly reach for your **shiv**.

Lovelorn and left out on **Valentine's Day**? Just pick up a box of children's themed cards, and play **cupid** while handing them out to people you encounter today. Do not worry about true love pairings; **divorce** solves all those messy mistakes.

When making plans, treat all **friends** as if they might be the companion/date/love of your life. You most certainly would not rearrange a first date with your dreamy **lover** for a last-minute, seemingly better opportunity with your co-worker's **mother-in-law**, would you? Just use the same ladylike/gentlemanly ways with your friends as with your **dates**, and you will always have numerous pals fighting to be first on all of your guest lists.

When dealing with an over-man-scaped **Lothario** who salaciously sends you unwelcome winks to make his **oh-so-subtle** points, simply wink back, and ask about his favorite esthetician. Sharing notes about skincare sends any hints of his remaining **testosterone** out the proverbial window.

Should you be asked out by someone who is **blissfully** unaware of your disinterest, feign hurt and shock as you respond, ***"Darling, we went out to dinner four years ago."*** Raise one eyebrow, slowly shake your head, or simply sigh as you **sashay** away.

Forget someone's **name** while making an introduction at a party, inauguration, or **symposium**? Simply call the unknown person by the first name that pops into your empty head . . . and watch how quickly you are **corrected**. Kindly tell this dear soul that they might think about **changing** their name to the new one—for an improved **numerology** frequency.

When offering to play **matchmaker** for **Auntie**, please remember that it is best if the suitor hails from nearly the same **generation**, speaks the same language, and has the ability to laugh himself **silly**. Having the same type of hair does not count, even if he does add **highlights** to his base color.

Things rocky on the **marital** front? Keep a **personal** log of complaints, but never air them publicly. Do not discuss your pet peeves, likes, **dislikes**—we all know that no long-term change ever really occurs. The only reason to go for **marriage** counseling is if you want a divorce. **Auntie** knows that the best marriage counselor is an ironclad **pre-nup**.

Feeling **overwhelmed**, but don't feel that any self-help program is a good fit for your **particular** issue? Start your own 12-Step program, counseling group, or religion. Invite all of your clients and **friends** to the initial meeting, and then watch as your personal popularity soars. Having an entourage always provides an immediate boost to one's **self-esteem**.

Auntie knows that **revenge** is best served cold. In fact, **Auntie** serves her revenge so very cold, it is politely offered up in a goblet that has been stored in the **freezer** for a year or two, with a hearty serving of icy shards in the mix. Just enough to turn your **lips** arctic blue, but not quite cold enough to induce instant **death**.

When you're **dating**, going over the top is a spectacular thing: **compliments**, words of love, and the intriguing wink are all quite **lovely**. But going over the top before you've even met someone is . . . dare I say it . . . off-putting and **scary**. How do you know that someone is truly wonderful, **gorgeous**, handsome, witty, smart, and funny until you have actually met?

Some people are **off-beat**; others are simply **insane**. It can be loads of fun to be around either group—the trick is to **escape** from the **relationship** before the insane begin to take themselves at their own **word**.

Feeling as if you **give**, and give, and give again, yet no one seems to realize or recognize you for your **efforts**? Remember, darling, charity does indeed begin at home, so be **charitable** to yourself once in a while. After giving to Sissy and Cousin Jasper, remember to give yourself something even if it is just a pat on the back or a glass of really yummy **Prosecco**. How can you possibly continue to help others if you do not help **yourself**?

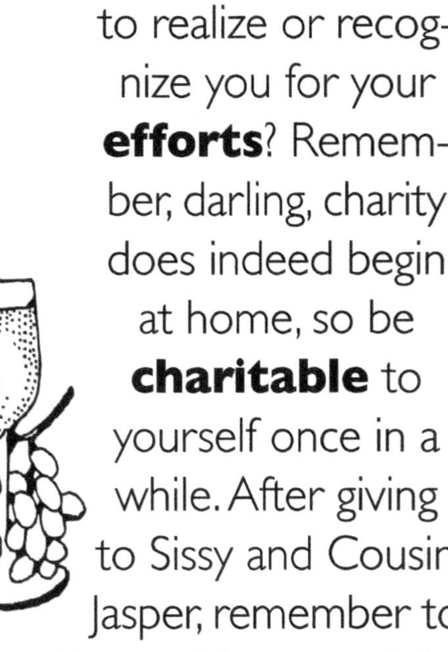

Be wary of those who claim to have a **spectacular** sense of humor, or who brag about their talent for **repartée**—often, such people will have an extremely negative response when the wit and **humor** is directed their way. Just a little ***"tit for tat"*** and ***"dish it out/can't take it"*** reminder.

Having a hard time dealing with **phonies**, liars, cheaters, and their kind? Throw caution to the wind, and dare to tell them the **truth**. They probably won't believe anything you say . . . and that, my **darlings**, is a bit of **gold**. Continue by telling the pretty little liar that she's not only **talented**, but is also on her way to winning some kind of industry **statuette**.

No, darlings, that comment you **overheard** was not at all mean: it was simply the unvarnished **truth**, said without an ounce of malice. Indeed, it was witty and sharp and **honest**. Simply learn to connect the dots as presented to you in life. One day, you just might be able to accept the picture that ultimately **reveals** itself. You may also want to discuss your **issues** with your shrink, sponsor, or **self-esteem** coach.

Telling us the story of your teen-age **daughter's** coming-of-age definitely qualifies you as an over sharing **mother**—even if you are doing so on a cleverly hidden internet site. Would you tell this story at a **State** Dinner, or while accepting a nationally recognized award? If not, then save the share for your **personal** diaries. By saving those shares, you are not only salvaging many a **friendship**—you are also saving your child from permanent humiliation, and the need for counseling. In this case, it is indeed the mother's fault. Of course, if the share is truly unique enough, we just might be able to get you a **two-picture** deal.

Here's a practical little reminder: just as the **bread** plate goes to your left, while your **drink** goes to your right, your current **beau** should always be within arm's length, while his **ex-wives** and girlfriends should always be in another **zip code**.

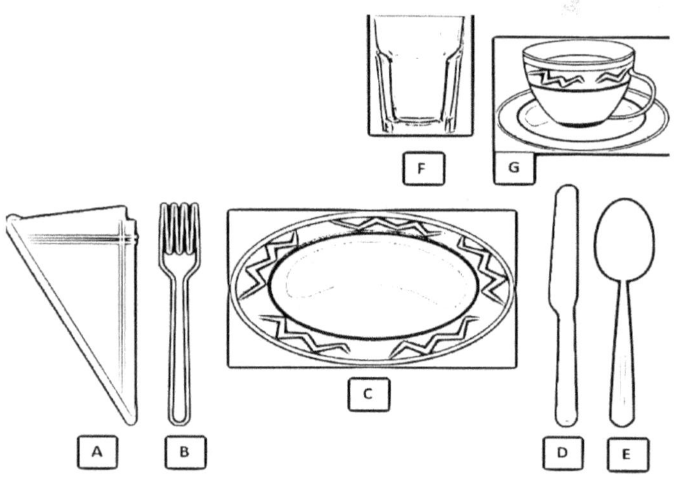

Auntie has no idea why any man would want to take his **wife's** name. What a silly, backward, anti-femme idea. Perhaps **Auntie** should say that she would never become the wife of a man who wanted to take her name. That is just a backward world. We need to move ahead, **darlings**, so become Mr. and Mrs. and be done with the name mess. More evidence for **Auntie's** side: How many teen boys doodled their names enmeshed with their **crush's** names, while pretending to calculate a cosine and tangent? Now you do the **math**.

Is a **humorless**, suffering soul forcing you to explain or justify your every witticism, bon mot, or good **mood**? Politely free yourself from the tyranny of their friendship; as a parting **gift**, offer the names of some self-help groups, medications, or **cocktail** recipes. Someday, he or she may realize that we well-adjusted folk have **feelings** too.

Is there a **crazy** person following you around, emailing, ranting, unable to see the **error** of her ways? Become a sweet Southern **belle** for a moment, and respond to her with the ever-so-passively polite ***"Bless your heart."*** Watch the craziness escalate . . . and, **voilà!**—the next chapter of your thriller is quickly completed.

Here's an easy way to get rid of those hangers-on. Keep a mini **voodoo** paper doll (easily made using an old photo or free hand drawing) in your purse or shirt pocket; and when the **pesky** person comes a bit too near, simply start **sticking** the voodoo paper doll with anything sharp that happens to be nearby. Not only will you keep the evil vibes away, it makes for a great **conversation** starter with the nice folk already seated **around** you.

On **Valentine's Day,** or any day, if you should bump into the current **wife** or girlfriend of a former **sweetie**, never stammer, avoid, or rue the day you left. When parting after such an encounter, give a naughty/salacious

wink, and remark, ***"give him a big kiss for me."*** **Auntie** is rarely passive-aggressive, but my darlings, there are exceptions to every **rule**.

Are things not quite going your way in your job, **relationship**, or family reunion? Just start issuing your personal brand of executive **orders**—it does not matter if anyone adheres to any of your **edicts**, and it does not matter if your orders are ethical. Ultimately, you will feel better—and we all know that it is simply about you, and only you. No one else really matters. Except **Auntie**, of course.

When on a blind **date**, if you should find yourself stuck in conversation with a **clueless**, bullying, arrogant-for-no-good-reason bore, use this interaction as a means of looking at how those without **moral** fiber behave. Chances are, you will never again encounter such an uncivil lout in your life. **Innocently** interview/prod/goad. If you should **inadvertently** anger this damaged creature, take thorough mental notes for a character in your next best-selling murder mystery. Remember; never let a rude soul steal anything from your **gracious** heart.

When in **public**, if you should be engaged in a mad, passionate, or achingly sweet embrace or **kiss**, be sure to **slyly** check for surveillance cameras, drones, or snoopy neighbors. **Privacy**, as we knew it just a few years ago, no longer exists. However, if you should be **lucky** enough to observe a high-profile A-lister in such a situation it's best to snap your **photos** quickly—so that you can be first in line to collect a high finder's fee from a tabloid, website, or **governmental** agency.

If you should find yourself in the company of a nonstop **nonsense** talker, simply press your personal **Mute** button on a seen or unseen pocket-sized remote **control**. Any electronic device, real or imagined, can be used for this purpose. Simply aim your real or mimed device at the inane **chatter-box** while saying, ***"click, click"*** out loud. With the dear soul on silent, you no longer have to respond or feign interest—just smile and nod while thinking about your growing bank account, an upcoming vacation, or your unerring sense of **style**.

Has your **lighthearted** point of view caused some dreary dullards to tell you to **"grow up"??** Remember to never ever allow those **unimaginative** ones to influence your joie de vivre, and darlings, please, we are begging you, to be **brave** enough to only grow up in the areas of your life where it is **absolutely** necessary.

When you are phoned up by a dear **soul**, and they chatter on, without a single **query** as to your well-being, followed by an abrupt ending of the call with the phrase, ***"I'm going to let you go,"*** one must only wonder about the validity of your **friendship**. End the relationship much more quickly by saying, ***"It's not me, it's you,"*** or vice versa as you hang up the phone and then **block** their number.

Auntie wants you to know that disagreement does not equate to being **evil**, stupid, or mean. If we disagree, and you present **logical**, sensible **arguments** for your point, you just might **earn** our respect. Name-calling, however, especially in lieu of civil discourse, is a waste of **Auntie's** time.

No, **darlings**, there never will come a time when the phrase ***"boys will be boys"*** ceases being useful. Instead of complaining, simply respect **men** for the creatures that they are—and then **calculate** the number of coven members required for your spells to take effect.

If you should find yourself being **underappreciated** by anyone, at any time, it is best to **immediately** cut ties to the useless oaf. Why on Earth would you ever spend a single second of your life among those who are not **grateful** to be in your presence, and **unaware** of your obvious charms? And please don't tell **Auntie** it is a self-esteem issue.

Have a **Queen** with a bee in his or her bonnet making unnecessarily **nasty** remarks about your lovely, happiness-filled life? Answer all comments without guile, but with a big grin—as you **patiently** wait for an answer from this envious soul. Chances are you will be waiting a **very** long time.

Find yourself befuddled/shocked/ appalled by an **offhand** remark from a **newfound** or long-time acquaintance. Perhaps it's time to reconsider the relationship. **Darlings**, you must know that sometimes, all it takes is one comment to figure out that some-one is **insane**, not a match, or ready to be locked up.

Auntie is seeing quite a bit of **stone-throwing** these days, and would like to remind you **darlings** that despite your quick wit and mighty strength . . . your houses . . . they are still made of **glass**. Hard to believe, is it not? Only throw stones if your own house is **properly** secured—or if you no longer want to be in contact with your **victims**.

Want to rid yourself of some unnecessary **hangers-on**? Simply say, ***"I told you so,"*** when anyone goes against your wishes. Very few things are as annoying as someone who **gloats**, and then gloats again or says something akin to, ***"Did we not already discuss this?"*** Remember to use these phases **carefully**—one time too many and you become the annoying one.

Auntie wants to encourage everyone to live their own fairy tale—fight the evil **queen**, slay (real and imagined) **dragons**, and find your true love. No one else can live your **life**—so it's up to you to make it as exciting as you choose—and always remember to expect a happy **ending**.

Trying to help an ungrateful bitch?

Don't.

1. When at a dinner party, where do you place the butter knife and your hubby's ex-girlfriend?

2. When is the mute button best put to use?

3. When dating, proper time to go "over the top" is:

    a. First date
    b. Third date
    c. Before meeting

Chapter III

Employment

With so many career changes and past employers, Auntie (modestly, of course) has come to think of herself as a bit of an expert in the area of jobs. She's proud to claim that she's never been fired—except for that part-time college job that was so very dreary—but instead, Auntie became so very bored that she had to quit or risk brain death.

Yes, we all must pay the rent, buy food, clothes, and a good cabernet—but really, if we are lucky enough to be living this life, shouldn't we allow ourselves to be employed somewhere that satisfies us just a little? Auntie thinks so—and thinks you deserve fulfillment at work too.

While on your **commute** to work, should you find yourself **weeping** uncontrollably, getting lost en route, or plotting the **murder** of your **boss**, it may be time to consider a career change. **Dramatic** exits from a wretched work environment will be a welcome diversion for your soon-to-be **ex-colleagues**.

In a **meeting-from-hell**? Use one of those clown lapel flowers that squirt water, and keep things lively by **aiming** for specific body parts of other attendees. Keep **score**, hits v. misses . . . you will be surprised at how much **fun** meetings become.

Handholding and career counseling can be so much **fun**. The next time you spend hours on the **phone** with your stuck-in-a-rut pal, send a little note of encouragement with a neatly typed **invoice** for your session fee tucked inside. You probably won't get **paid**, but they probably won't complain (or talk) to you again. It becomes a real-life **win-win** situation.

Auntie would like to share a secret she learned from her dear **Daddy**: If you should be involved in an argument or **lawsuit**, and the other side concedes a point **stop** and acknowledge your **win**, and then move on to your next point. Continuing to **argue** further to prove how wrong or **idiotic** your foe is will not help you in any way. It may even cause additional **irrational**, non-winnable points to be **conjured** up.

Want a **license** to poke your nose into everyone's business at will? Simply **attach** the word ***"Consultant"*** to your name, and head out into the world. Catch the image of someone who needs a neck lift or **blepharoplasty**? Use tact when offering beauty tips as a Cosmetic Surgery **Consultant**. Spy a basket at the grocer's full of all the wrong kind of foodstuffs? Toss a few **dining** tips to the shopper—now you're a Nutrition **Consultant**. See an **overzealous** amateur designer wearing too many floral prints? Quickly end that trend in your capacity as a Clothing **Consultant**. Be kind and **gentle** when offering all this free advice—remember, not everyone will appreciate your **wise** and knowing eye.

If you are lucky enough to have possession of a **business** card or means of contacting **Auntie** Jodi, this certainly does not give you license to add that **email** address to your hideously boring daily **newsletter**. **Auntie** does not give a whit about your next gig, seminar, **political**, sexual, or philosophical orientation, or how you plan to market yourself into the next tax bracket. **Auntie's** card does not belong on the email equivalent of the ***"win a free lunch"*** fishbowl at TGIFriday's.

If you feel the need to **brag** about your career, children, spouse, **book** deal, weight loss, income stream, sexual **conquests**, or other such subject, survey your audience **before** launching into your spiel. Chances are that you, dear **soul**, are the only one who is truly interested. **Yawn**.

Auntie abhors all things smug. There really is no reason for this point of view. It is **obnoxious**, pretentious, and unkind. Smug seems to be the **worst** variety of that **falsely** superior attitude so many people have assumed these days, due to their **lack** of graciousness. If you should meet someone who is condescending or smug, **simply** remember your own upbringing, your noblesse oblige—and then attack the smug one with anything nearby that has a sharp edge—**preferably** your own brain.

Dealing with an **alleged** business pro who uses **happy-face**

emoticons when corresponding? Cut through the smiley stuff by ending your notes with non-smiley statements such as, ***"My cat died,"*** or ***"Today's the tenth anniversary of my grandfather's death."*** Expect to receive a frownie face back in the **response**.

If you're supplying advice, counsel, or a **shoulder** to cry on to many a friend or acquaintance, then it's high time you start calling yourself a **Coach**. There are so many options out there: Life Coach, **Dating Coach**, Investment Coach, Find-Your-Life-Passion Coach. Just print up some business cards, and go for it. Chances are you know more than many a **soul** with **fancy** letters tagging along after their names–and in comparison, your advice will, most likely, be much more **valuable** and heartfelt.

If the **enormity** of a particular project is giving you the **blues**, take the opportunity to put your current frame of mind to good use. Write **lyrics** for a melancholy love song, ballad, or jazzy wail. Find a musician, and post the tune on a pay-for-play site—not only will you be making some **money** with your creative gloominess, you'll probably become a viral **superstar** with a huge book deal, and all the most **attractive** people will want to be your friends . . . though you'll now have another career/project to **worry** about.

Auntie wants you to know that lying, cheating, or stealing is never acceptable. If you **steal** her hints, her trinkets, or anything else of tangible or intangible **value**, you will be found—not just by **Auntie's** attorneys, but also by **Auntie** herself. Attorneys file papers and work within the law; **Auntie** does not.

Feeling **nauseated** about the April 15th day of government **thievery**? Whether your funds are earned or **inherited**, remember that all of us payers are somewhat **distraught**. We would never get political, and do not have the **necessary** licenses to advise about being overtaxed—we always rely upon our **CPA**, our business manager, and **Glenfiddich**.

Networking with a group that is obviously not of a **similar** mind-set? Always make sure the name written on your sticky **nametag** is legible. No need to use your given name, an alias/nom de guerre/ stage name always makes an early exit less stressful, and greatly **diminishes** the odds of being tracked down by anyone in the **organization**.

Bored or **overwhelmed** with facts, figures, and poll results? Ignore the **so-called** experts, and start your own polling firm, so you may query the masses about life's really **important** and meaningful questions. Always remember to start by delving into an **acquaintance's** insights about you—it is nice to have the honest statistics about your true **intelligence**, grace, beauty, and wit close at hand—which are quite helpful for quick **reference** during those rare moments of self-doubt.

Don't ever think that your childhood years playing **Monopoly**, chess or **Jacob's Ladder** were a waste of time. Life skills—such as wealth accumulation, outsmarting your **boss**, or using rope to trip or strangle a **pathologically** evil acquaintance—will always be of value. That and target practice at your favorite **shooting** range.

Feeling left out during **Pageant** Season? Do your best to fit in by going to a **local** fabric store and purchasing a long **swatch** of satin in a nice color that brings out your eye color or skin tones. **Drape** it across your torso, emblazoned with the **title** of your favorite national/international/fictional charity. Remember to always carry a decorated tin for **donations**; a smile and thank you do wonders. Watch as your gown fund/person-al **endowment** quickly grow.

If a surly **clerk** is giving you below-par service, remember to always **treat** those who work for you with respect—the quickest way to counter a bad **attitude** is to incredulously, yet kindly mirror back their words, but with your own spin. If you've been told that ***"I'm going to go out of my way for you,"*** immediately and calmly repeat back, ***"you're going out of your way for me, Dear?"*** Then just stare at the clerk's nametag as you watch **squirming** ensue.

When **faced** with too much to do, simply think of all your work as **empire-building**. I am currently building my own empire. I am, of course, **Empress** Jodi, but I also like the sound of **Czarina Zhodee**, and HRH Jodi I. When creating your **fantasy** world, never let facts weigh you down.

Unfamiliar **soul** at work using overly sarcastic, friendly, or fake phrases such as, ***"dear, hon/ honey, or sweetie"*** when addressing you? Simply echo back the fake **endearment** each time the word is tossed your way, and watch how quickly the dolt wakes up. Make sure you use the same dismissive **intonation** when repeating the phony terms—a **sucker** punch is much more easily administered with a heartfelt and **sincere** smile.

Out-of-balance friend offering up **unsolicited** suggestions about harmonizing your energy fields? Avoid an **unnecessary** chakra alignment by offering her some balancing suggestions of your own that **involve** assets/liabilities and profit/loss statements. Chances are this dear friend is **math-phobic**, so watch as the energy quickly shifts to meditating/medicating/ Merlot during your accounting recitation. This is **known** as a perfectly **balanced** case of two birds/one stone.

The next time someone tells you of their grand and glorious plans for their **career**, marriage, spouse, or children, instead of trying to tell them they are living in a fantasy world or **lying** to themselves simply nod, and offer up a bit of true fantasy philosophy, such as ***"you only succeed if your undies are inside-out,"*** or ***"always use a knife when you need a spoon."*** They will undoubtedly believe **you**.

Help have the night off? **Auntie** is not at all helpless in the kitchen, and here's a **hint**: neither are you. Use your creative flair to create a one-of-a kind **dinner**. Tonight's inspiration: ratatouille.

Let them all think that you can't tell a ramekin from a **radish**. . . and then surprise everyone, because as with your life, your **cooking** adventures really don't need a **recipe**.

Worried about **finances** and your future? Join legions of fundraisers, and start your own **political** action committee—or perhaps you might start a charity in your name, as many **athletes** have done. If you are worried about **government** intervention and regulations—just think positive thoughts—and **voilà**, all those pesky rules disappear. Add a personal touch by sending out ***"Thank you for your contribution"*** cards within a week of any monetary deposit. It is still important to be polite, especially if you are writing from inside a **prison** cell.

Are you **fighting** the urge to spew vile words about some ex-lover, former boss, or **erstwhile** friend? Unless the information is of a **caliber** that would entice the editors of **TMZ** or some such organization, save yourself from public humiliation or a **lawsuit** thusly: Change the players' names, and write down all the **juicy** little tidbits for inclusion in your upcoming **novella**. You must however, pinky swear and remember to call **Auntie** to share all the real, sordid details before the first edition is released.

Yes, **darlings**, you can fix some things on your own—and be entrepreneurial at the same time. **Auntie** Jodi is so proud of herself: while trouble-shooting a **computer** problem all by herself, she was amazed that she could fix the issue on her own. If plugging in all those look-alike black wires takes an engineering degree, **Auntie** now has a Ph.D. She is setting up an online degree **program** of her own; with diplomas that are tastefully designed. Take note—all **diplomas** will be sent out—as soon as the enrollment fees are paid—**in full**.

Give yourself a **title**. No, not the usual Mr., Miss, Mrs., or Dr.—**rather**, something that aligns with your current frame of mind, skills or interests. I personally know a Mayor of **Awesomeville**, a Prince of Impolite Banter, a Queen of **Parallel** Parking, the General Contractor to all of **Beverly Hills**, and of course the Baron of Cheap **Cabernets**. How would you like to be addressed?

Auntie does not believe in burning bridges; however, **it** may sometimes become necessary to verbally singe a few edges as you **gracefully** exit from an unfriendly or unkind work, personal, or online environment.

Is there an overly **zealous** do-gooder in your life who is **trying** to get you to a team-building **exercise**, a log cabin retreat, a hand-holding ***"share"*** session, or an icebreaker for some darling new charity? Inform the **altruistic** one that you only team up with those you personally deem **worthy**, you will gladly retreat to a log cabin if there is room service, and that you gladly welcome all ice-breakers that are accompanied by a glass and some lovely **vodka** and tonic.

Whenever necessary, **darlings**, one may need to pick up the slack, take charge, and **assume** a leadership role. This applies to almost all aspects of your life. Is there anything **worse** that an ersatz leader who fumbles and **futzes** around at the podium, dais, or boudoir? Instead of day-dreaming about your upcoming trek around the continent, become a **Leader of Men** and watch how the stressed instantly relax while appreciating your polite **assertiveness**.

Feel like a **slave** to someone else's dreary/robotic **hallucinations**? Never ever allow your dreams and wishes to be given second-class **status**. It's simply a matter of priorities, **darlings**—and who says your needs are not as important as the next fellow? Certainly not **Auntie**.

1. When should you quit a job that makes you weep?

2. What type of skill sets do you have for a new career as a Coach?

3. Come up with two believable names to use for networking nametags.

Chapter IV

Socializing

Is there anything drearier than a bad party, clueless host, or useless soiree companion? Well, in reality there might be...but Auntie is speaking about the dear souls who are so wrapped up in their own shyness or braggadocio that they don't even realize that the whole point of the event is, yes, socializing? Does anyone even know what that means anymore?

Here are some tips on having a marvelous time at every event you attend—if you're reading this, you probably already have a great time wherever you go—so maybe you might share some of these with a friend...

When someone asks your **sign**, just make it up—and, yes, they will tell you how much you are like your **fictional** sign. That's just one of the ways I amuse myself when attending a **soirée**. Today I'm a **Taurus**.

Auntie Jodi knows your child is the most **adorable** creature to have ever been born—but **tantrums** at restaurants and screaming fits at department stores are, in reality, not so **cute**. Perhaps **Mummy** and Papa are the ones who need some home training—saying ***"no"*** early on might just prevent spawning yet another generation of the overly and **unjustly** entitled brat-child-parent **cycle**.

Feel like telling a **dinner** guest that they left clear-thinking logic in some cloudy **situation** room? Become a dinnertime diplomat, and smile as they **spew** their incredible **nonsense**. Answer back with a few wacky true facts, and before **renewing** the friendship or issuing another **invitation**, make a formal request for their visas the next time they attempt to cross the **threshold** into your home. It is just good policy, n'est pas?

Find yourself **embroiled** in a **deliciously** dull conversation at **yet** another art opening/wedding/state dinner? It is **advised** that everyone learn a few phrases in an **obscure** language—it is so much more **polite** and erudite to insult someone when language is an issue. Remember to **smile** knowingly while nodding your head when exiting from the somnambulant **clique**.

Darlings, if you are going to make an attempt at a **humorous** retort, make sure your response does not need to be explained to your **audience**. We all know that the only result of such **clarification** is an embarrassingly loud thud.

Has the owner of a home with **not-so-clean** carpets asked you to remove your shoes before crossing the threshold into her lovely **abode**? Unless this is a well-known ethnic/family custom that would throw the embassy's **protocol** minister into a tizzy, you are allowed to **politely** ignore this request while keeping your tootsies inside your shoes. When inviting a guest into your **home**, the idea is to make them feel **welcome**—not immediately ask them to **disrobe**. Unless, of course, it is a disrobing kind of party—and in that case, bring plenty of **disinfectant**.

When **discussing** the popularity of movies, media-types, and **moguls**, let your tablemates dither on for as long as possible before letting them all know that your **personal** approval rating is the highest it has been in seven years. Smile as you inquire into their **untallied** totals—sipping on a good Cabernet always helps to ease the **tedium** of their responses.

If you should be seated at a dinner **party** next to a know-it-all who in reality knows very **little**, begin your conversation with the following phrase: ***"Nine out of ten people surveyed agree with the idea that..."*** It does not matter if no one agrees with you, and it does not matter if you are telling the **truth**. Just remember to use that simple **phrase**, because no one checks facts these days—facts really are oh-so-very **tedious**.

Every once in a **while**, have a day where you tell off/read the riot act to/give an **honest** analysis to all the takers and fakers in your world. No need to be **polite**--but refrain from using profanity--just this once--it dulls your argument. **Auntie** guarantees that not only will you feel better; you will undoubtedly have a wonderful few **stories** to tell.

Out-of-control wild **child** being ignored by overly indulgent, talking, texting, **emotionally** needy parents in public? When the sweet little **dervish** comes begging for your attention, ply him with sugar, caffeine or **alcohol** before sending him/her back to Mommy.

It may take a **village**, but **darling**, we are not even the same **tribe**.

Everyone needs to **create** or adopt a standard/stock response to what one perceives to be a **ridiculous** statement. **Auntie's** current favorite: **Pfft**. This word works well in person as well as in print, and can be used in an **encouraging** or disdainful way—as a stand-alone response, or incorporated into a **snappy** retort. The key here—as always—is in the **delivery**.

When **dealing** with a fundraising event that includes a mix of A-listers, and B-C-D-listers, there is no need to call **attention** to the varying ranks of attendee **importance**. Labeling one group the "VIPs" will not do much to help you increase your coffers with those non-VIPs. Depending on the **attendees**' sense of humor, you might try labeling one group The Wealthy Ruling Elite, another The **Pompous** Tastemakers, and yet another The **Drunken** Idiots. What fun your gathering will be! Remember, we are all **VIPs**—in one group or another.

When **deluged** with holiday party invitations, remember that after **accepting** a given invite it is incredibly crass to cancel the first R.S.V.P. when a **seemingly** better summons comes along. The only exception to this cancellation rule would be for your own **elopement**(s). When conveying your regrets, remember to tell the disappointed hostess that she will, of course, be invited to your **marriage** reception—as you **blushingly** mention the names of the shops where you are registered.

If you should find yourself **stuck** in conversation with a dear soul who will **not** let you leave—asking yet another leading question, **hanging** on your arm, or using your kindness as a means of avoiding their **particular** brand of weekly anonymous meeting—quickly end the **tête-à-tête** by placing your fist to your chest while uttering the actors' saving grace, ***"and, scene."*** After bowing, you are now free turn on your **heel** and head for the bar.

When asked to remind a long-lost **acquaintance** of your given name, and after doing so, should this dear acquaintance utter ***"that's right"*** or some equally irksome phrase when stating your moniker, **Auntie** suggests you think again about renewing this **relationship**. Of course, you are right—it is your name. What an absolutely **ridiculous** remark. What is wrong are those **annoying** people who tell you you're right when you **already** know how right you really are.

Auntie is **aghast**. She was recently accused of being **polite** in public to a dear soul who has very different **beliefs**. **Darlings**, this should be ***Helpful Hint #1***—it never hurts to be polite to everyone (at least in **mixed** company). Remember--save all your snark, biting satire, and **lampooning** for the stage or lively conversations with **trusted** pals. You just never know when **"*they*"** are listening.

If you're feeling a bit **restless** at your next celebration, offer to take other guests on the **Royal** Tour of the house/condo/apartment. Yes, this can be on your first visit to the **abode**. Walk through the place, pointing out interesting **paintings** or pieces of furniture in each room. Use your best **tour** guide voice, and when noting items of interest, remember to ask guests for a thumbs-up or thumbs-down **regarding** the decor.

Tell the small-talk **challenged** party guests you're psychic, and watch what happens! Give free **holiday** readings to all party-goers. No, you don't have to really be psychic. You can usually say something like, ***"You've been somewhat frustrated by your work and feel that if given the chance, you could bring quite a bit more creativity into the mix."*** Or you could knowingly nod and say, ***"people don't always know how thoughtful you really are, do they?"***

If you **smile** at your fellow party-goers, they'll probably smile back; some might even **amble** over to chat. Unless, of course, everyone is wearing **black** and is just too **cool** for the room. In that case, pretend you are Wednesday Addams, and skulk around . . . you'll be very popular. Merry **Merry**!

When faced with a conversation **manipulator** who uses the phrases such as, ***"you agree that..."*** or ***"you can see why we need to do that..."*** remember that you can stop this amateur psycho-babbler in his or her tracks with the simple response, ***"No, not really."*** Remember to smile, keeping a **quizzical** expression on your face, while holding fast to those three words of polite disagreement. You will always win your point—especially when you hold fast to the reality of the situation.

Awkward with introductions? Go for the two-cheek air **kiss** when meeting someone new. Do not ever actually plant your **lips** on anyone's face—that is an obvious sign of a rank **amateur**.

You can tell them you picked up the habit from a friend who summered on the **Continent**. Speak in a thick French or Italian accent. **Ciao**, baby.

If you should find yourself waking up on your hosts' settee after **celebrating** with them, always remember to leave a small gratuity tucked under a nearby **knickknack**. Depending on the accommodations, it is customary to leave between $2 and $7 per **night**. If you only have large bills, do not ask for **change**.

Whispering fools talking about you across the table at a dinner **party**? Laughingly instruct these rude **plebeians** that a hand positioned in front of the mouth with a **deadhead** gaze in anyone's direction is the **epitome** of gauche. Then demonstrate using a stage **sotto** voce tone, saying things such as ***"that woman with the ugly haircut has herpes,"*** or ***"her son is a drug addict because she smoked dope in the home."*** Remember to summon your driver to bring the car around before the next round of **rumors** begins.

Have you received an invitation to some sort of ghastly **reunion**? The only reasons to go are to show everyone how **fabulous** you look, because you have a **prestigious** career, or if you've become incredibly rich. Even if you are remarkably unaccomplished, you are **certainly** welcome to attend, but make sure to wear dark **sunglasses** at all times. And this is fun—immediately tell all **attendees** that they haven't changed a bit—makes for a unique **conversation** starter. It is only after you've been chatting the other attendee up a bit than you can **politely** inquire as to their name.

At a meet-and-greet, but not feeling too **meety** or **greety**? Take out a pen, and offer to sign the programs, menus or **napkins**. No my **sweet**, you do not have to use your real name—it is best if the signature is **illegible**. If anyone asks, wink and tell them you are a **writer**.

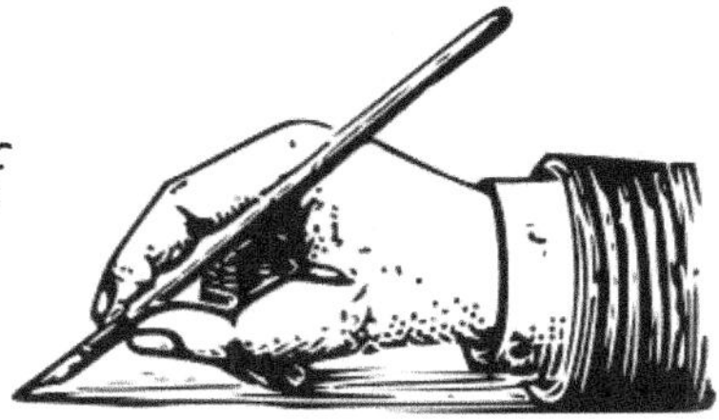

Heading to an **award** ceremony? Looking good takes careful planning. Make sure all **Botox** touch ups are completed at least three weeks before you stroll down the **red** carpet. Four weeks and you'll be a **photog's** dream.

Auntie thinks this should, in reality, be ***Helpful Hint #1***: Always trust your gut. Always listen to your **gut**. If you think someone is putting a **gossamer** mist over the truth, you're probably right, and they probably are. **Crap**, my darlings, is crap. Listen. Be still. Then kick the disgusting, lying **brats** in the belly, show them the door, and **disinfect** any surface they may have **touched**.

When faced with overly **prying**, intrusive, or meddling queries, simply respond with the **evil** eye, a raised **eyebrow**, or a blank stare. Then turn and **sashay** away. Not only does this give the Access Hollywood, National Enquirer, **TMZ**, and People Magazine poseur snoops a reason to pause—and possibly think—it also makes for a great **cover** shot.

Using words with **double** meanings is a sure-fire hit at a party. **Amuse** yourself by mentioning to your party **mates** that your **Tranny** is on the fritz. Whether car lovers or **cross-dressers**, you will quickly make loads of new **friends**.

Worried about singeing off your **eyelashes** with some not-so-safe-and-sane **fireworks**? Remember: all types of sparklers are de **rigueur** for any type of celebration, especially when we are talking about our independence, **liberty**, and freedom. **Auntie** does love it when the sky crackles with July 4th festivities and when her beau presents her with a new sparkly, celebratory **bauble**.

Conversation at a lull while at a **formal** dinner? Convince your table mates to do ***"the wave"*** whenever the help enter with another course. While sipping sherry and nibbling on a petit **macaroon**,

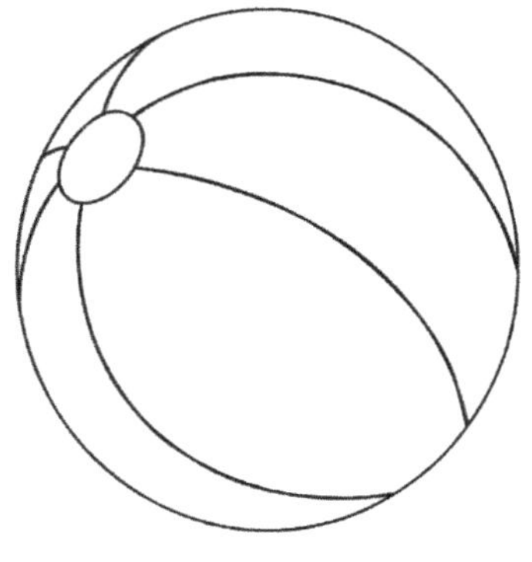

keep the fun going by pulling out an **inflatable** beach ball to volley around.

While chatting at a **cocktail** party, should you find yourself staring at a **painting** that is hanging at a not-quite-right angle, **divulge** to a few that you've recently become **feng shui-certified**. Watch the excitement mount as you direct your fellow party-going minions to **adjust** the listing artwork. When finished, encourage the crowd to **inhale** deeply, and admire the room's improved **energy** flow.

Is a manner-less **buffoon** asking overly nosy questions? Make good use of the non sequitur: ***"Q. How old are you? A. 34D." "Q. What was your net income last year? A. Tampons." "Q. You're not married? A. Ecclesiastes 3:7, or Proverbs 10:19."*** Always remember to flash a **sincere** smile when responding.

If an open-minded **free-thinker** says something along the lines of, ***"she doesn't even look Jewish/black/Mexican/etc."*** make her actually try to think by simply responding, ***"like me?"*** Alternately, ***"describe what that looks like."*** Watch as squirming and back-pedaling ensue.

Have a few **pals** who double-book themselves so that their positive R.S.V.P. actually means ***"I'll work the room for ten minutes, then escape to a VIP party"***? Entice them to stay by holding a carnival-style raffle at your next **soirée**, handing out tickets upon their arrival. Wait until after dessert to announce the **winning** number, and make the grand prize worthwhile—perhaps that little investment cottage that's now an **underwater** fixer-upper.

Overzealous party-goer snapping unauthorized candid photos with their new camera/phone/gadget? **Corral** those amateur **paparazzi** by whipping out your camera to fight fire with fire. Make sure your shots of them are as **unflattering** as possible... extortion can be so much fun.

Auntie Jodi is thrilled to be getting all of these **fabulous** invitations to online events. Her **dance** card is absolutely overflowing. If only she actually knew the kind people who were so **graciously** inviting her to join in the festivities. It might be even more exciting if she were actually interested in all the **darling** little details of your life.

Auntie understands **sarcasm**, but when meeting someone for the first time you may want to hold off on showing off all your **über-dry** wit. **Dullards** might think you are mean, lovelorn dates could see you as a **threat**, and **employers** are likely to immediately pull out the company handbook. Of course, all bets are off if you've **encountered** an equal—so go ahead and let the repartee begin. Just be careful that the quick-witted one is not covering for some childhood issues—unless you too are in **denial**.

Make your own ***"Naughty or Nice"*** list, but keep the requirements for inclusion a secret. At your next **holiday** party, hand out **symbolic** gifts or favors to each guest, while announcing that each item has special **significance** to each recipient. If a certain person needs to be taught a lesson, make that gift a **particularly** significant statement. When dealing with the dense or sensitive, it might be best to refrain from signing the ***"From"*** portion of the gift tag.

Darlings, we are all long-distance calls—so please find another **excuse** when you accidently pick up our call. Have a few **well-rehearsed**, less common reasons for cutting the **conversation** short—perhaps you and your personal chef are planning **vegan** appetizers, maybe you are signing a **lucrative** charity endorsement deal. Saying you are on a long-distance call is so very ho-hum, **1970s**, and rude.

What type of cotillion does one **graduate** from that allows the diner to rest their non-dominant arm on the **dining** table while shoveling food into their mouth with the **wrong** fork? It's not **breeding**, darlings—anyone who wants to learn can do so. We all know about keeping **elbows** off the table; that goes for forearms, **too**.

Darlings, just because you have something to add to a **scintillating** conversation does not mean that you need to **weigh** in right this second. Might I **suggest** that you listen in for a few moments before sharing your non **sequitur**? Discretion is, indeed, often the better part of conversational **valor**.

After responding in the **affirmative**, should you find yourself feeling less than **enthusiastic** about attending a party, concert, **inauguration**, or coronation, always send a personal note of **regret**—or, if need be, make a quick, last-minute phone call . . . **explaining** yourself to your hosts. Asking a friend who is attending to relay your **message** of incapacitation is not only rude, it is also **positively** dreary and oh-so-very-high school.

Are **nametags** being doled out at a **soirée** or premiere? Have a bit of fun, and use a nom de party

for that **sticky** little piece of paper. If another name does not **immediately** come to mind, simply write in the name of a little known author, silent film **star**, or jazz musician. Personal favorites include **Nellie** Bly, Pola Negri, and June **Christy**.

Chapter IV Quiz

1. What is the proper amount to tip the morning after sleeping it off on a friend's sofa?

2. Should wild children be given:

   a. Sugary food

   b. Alcoholic beverages

   c. Caffeinated beverages

   d. All of the above

3. What is one acceptable reason to graciously cancel an RSVP to a party?

Chapter V

The World

Everywhere we go, someone wants to rein us in, ruin our fun, or put us in our place (as if we need them to tell us), or make a new rule for a newly minted "wrong."

Well, there is no need to walk through your life scared of what other people have to say—Auntie would never recommend anyone be rude, but aren't they being rude to us?

Surrounded by the PC **police**? Want to have a private giggle? Ask the **PC** officer why he or she has those beliefs. **Scratch** your head, wrinkle up your nose or just act **confused**. Remember to always be **polite** when posing your query. Give them **30** seconds to explain. Of course, this works best if you have a second hand on your watch or a timer app on your phone. Shout, **"GO!"** when the official timing begins.

GO!

It is no longer necessary to pull out your **compact** and feign **lipstick** reapplication in order to see the annoying **gossips** sitting behind you at the neighborhood **bistro**. Your ubiquitous and completely unobtrusive cell phone camera can be utilized to help you remember these **lovely** ladies and their **trifling** conversation for a lifetime.

Find yourself in conversation with **pretentious** poseurs? Simply exclaim, ***"Sassy!"*** or ***"You go, Girl!"*** This allows you to gracefully **exit**, and it interrupts their convoluted **train** of thought.

Really, my **darlings**, if you have anything of **value** to add to our conversation, by all means, say it **aloud**—so we can all appreciate your wit, opinion, or **idiocy**. Mumbling responses are for nitwits, cowards and **dullards** . . . so do us all a favor, and keep that **mumbling** to yourself.

At a party with a bunch of **sincere**, **naïve** and incredibly dull do-gooders? Do your own good deed, and disagree (always **politely**) with every opinion or cause they stubbornly adhere/cling to. Keep **disagreeing** until the conversation becomes laughingly **silly**, ridiculous, or you find the inspiration for your next screenplay. Just for fun, give a **conspiratorial** wink to the unwitting leader of the opposition as you **exit** the salon.

Driver/**Chauffeur** have the day off? When swerving to avoid rear-ending the **texting** driver in front of you, always smile and wave when you drive alongside this texting **maniac**. As you pass, use discretion when determining the number of **fingers** to use as you wave.

Have you been told it's **rude** to disagree? Here is a **polite** way around that **silly** rule. If you should find yourself in conversation with a **dolt**, at an opportune time say, ***"That's a macro issue, I'm speaking on a micro level,"*** or vice-verse. This phrase generally stops them in their **tracks** and gives you a chance to shut the fools down. **Manners** do count.

Traffic got you down? Now is the time to use those long-ago learned **Morse** Code skills. Just toot the following combination as you **wait** behind someone who doesn't know how to make a left turn . . . or when a **driver** cuts you off while **changing** lanes, only to be found waiting at the red light on your approach. You'll feel better immediately! Now **kids**, go memorize this sequence:

..-. ..-

(Short horn blast for the **dot**—and of course, longer blast for the **dash**.)

If the **butler** has the night off, and you're racing through the **grocer's** looking for the perfect tin of caviar—don't forget, the rules of the **road** must be applied when pushing your cart. Move to the right, **signal** lane changes, and never **text** while trying to negotiate your way around the pre-cut **crudités**. Someone cut you off in aisle three? Not to worry—help them have more fun at **checkout**—just drop a few extra items into their cart when no one's looking. **Alcohol**, deodorant, or a rump roast are some of my favorite ***"toss-and-run"*** items.

Feeling as if you have lost your raison **d'être**? Just grab a clipboard and head out into the **world**. You will immediately be granted entry into all sorts of fun places. If anyone should start asking you **probing** questions, start taking notes as you give **vague** responses. Wearing a **jaunty** hat will give you that extra **flair**.

Carry a pack of **Post-It®** notes with you, so that you can leave behind short **helpful**

hints of your own. Hosts' kitchen a bit **sloppy**? Use the county **health** department code to rate the site. When leaving your letter critique **(A, B, or C)**, always remember to use good **penmanship**.

Keep using those **Post-it®** notes. Does the car next to you need some **parking** help? Put a **Post-it®** with your ever-so-thoughtful suggestions on their **windshield**, and of course, be polite. **Spelling** counts.

get more
post-it notes

Need to lose **weight** in a hurry for that **red** carpet photo-op next week? Simply contract a case of food **poisoning**, and boom—twelve pounds will be **gone** in only three days. Not only is it fast and easy—the best part is that there are no **silly** books to buy, food to measure, or **rules** to follow.

Feeling a bit **ignored** during **award** season? Put on your best evening **attire**, and head to a local **movie** theater. Position yourself at the entrance and thank all the **folks** for coming out to see you. Remember to bring along a **mini** bottle of hand sanitizer—thanking all of the ***"little people"*** can be a very **germy** business.

When **circumstances** are such that your only option is a public **restroom**, never ever jiggle the knob, should the door be **locked**. The poor **soul** using the facilities does not need to be **rushed**. If it really is an **emergency**, take out your pocket electric **screwdriver**, and remove the doorknob. Remember to be **polite**, and say ***"so sorry!"*** if you should catch the potty user in **mid-stream**.

When posing for a photo with a chatty and **adoring** fan, **concentrate** on the camera, not the dear fan's conversation. A good photo lasts **forever**...and the fan can always be cropped out at a **later** date.

Having a hard time suffering **fools** today? Answer all questions as **tersely** as possible. Remove all humor, wit, and **sarcasm** from your **retorts**. They still won't get it, but you'll be **elated** at how the befuddled **soul** makes for an even better foil. **En garde**!

Is the **over-coiffed** theatre patron sitting in the box next to you wearing enough **cloyingly** sweet, heady, or floral cologne to entice the **EPA** into yet another government-funded **pollution** study? Come prepared with color-coordinated **surgical** masks—imploringly ask your date/spouse to tie your mask on for you. **Remember** to reciprocate, and offer to **tie-up** your date/spouse later on.

Auntie Jodi would like to suggest that the **DMV** expand to cover **texting** pedestrians. That way, those of us **caught** behind someone who is not able to **simultaneously** walk and text will no longer have to avoid the dear one who has stopped in his/her tracks to **text**. Perhaps cell phones should come with an **app** that automatically flashes a white brake light behind all stalled-out **texters**.

Feeling as if you are not doing your part for the **community**? Simply offer to mentor a needy **soul**. It does not matter what the topic; you will be surprised at how any and all advice/**guidance**/leadership is welcomed. Common sense advice is best—especially for the **dears** with those **pesky** profound questions.

Once in a while, **swap** your responses to those front-porch **proselytizers** with those for your candidate-canvassers.

Cacophonous music blaring from the not-so-trendy **poseur's** open car window? Wave politely and ask the driver the name of the

performer, station, or **podcast** from which the noise is emanating. Suggest your own obscure Latin chart toppers—***"Te sunt stultus"*** or ***"Mordebit me"*** as you motor away.

Is a loud-mouthed **cell** phone user at the gym, grocery store, or hair salon **disturbing** you with her **neurotic** conversation and poor **syntax**? Quiet the annoying talker by boldly **entering** into the conversation. Supply witty and helpful retorts to anything you hear, and watch how quickly the **talker** lowers her volume, or—even better—puts the phone into your hands so you can **argue** her case.

Overwhelmed by **facts** from one side and fantasy from the other? Get into your personal **Dewey** Decimal mode, and think of it all as a trip to the library, bookstore, or **Amazon**. Use your instincts to label one as fiction, the other as **nonfiction**—do not be afraid to judge one as good and the other as bad. If we did not make **judgment** calls, then how would we know chic from trash, diamonds from colored glass, or cream from **non-fat**?

When faced with people who do not agree with you on **political** issues, state your point, followed by this phrase: ***"I'm Jodi Adler, and I approved this message."*** A reminder, **darlings**: you will want to use your own name when putting this phrase to use. If you are dealing with the **politically** deaf, do not bother trying to reason with them; just treat them like the **kindergarteners** they are—give them a big hug, and suggest a nap. Then pray that they forget to **vote**.

Not sure how to **vote** on any of those heavily skewed **ballot** measures, propositions, and popularity contests? **Auntie** does not like to get political—but will share her one and only secret to success in the **voting** booth: Check your opponent's ballot choices, and then simply vote the opposite way. **Remember**: the best way to educate yourself about the true **pitfalls** of any issue is to learn the opposition's point of view—**enabling** you to beat them at their own game.

See someone walking down the **boulevard** in a getup that begs for a major **intervention**? Be generous with your knowledge of color, texture, and **fashion**. Offer to **donate** your time to become their personal **stylist**. Not only will you be able to shop without

having to foot the bill, you will also be doing a **service** for all mankind—while overseeing a Pygmalion-like change in a grateful **soul**.

Tired of the everyday **misuse** and **overuse** of crass language and **swear** words? Thumb through a dictionary, and increase your **vocabulary** while you upscale your list of insults. Use classic and **archaic** words to ever-so-politely insult the idiots in your **midst**. Among my favorites: battleaxe, mooncalf, **harridan**, **virago**, ninny hammer, and harpy.

Watching a **parade**? Why not dress in the anticipated style of your favorite **float** or band? Remember—there will probably be some type of **queen** involved, so tiaras and feathers are your go-to accessories. If you happen to be a **drill** team or marching band alum, you are expected to point out the off-the-beat, out-of-line **steppers**.

Don't be one of those who proclaim that ***"I'm not into funerals."*** Few really are, unless you are a member of the **walking** dead. That, **darling**, is not what funerals are about. We go to **funerals** for all sorts of reasons: because we loved someone or because they meant something to us, or, as they say, ***"to pay our respects."*** Remember—if you cannot grant respect, you **certainly** won't command it.

Auntie prefers her **epithets** to be foreign sounding--and of the no-punches pulled variety. If you should try to **insult** someone by using words/phrases that are actually anti-insults (such as **straightforward**, bossy, or honest) you are probably not **aware** of the workings of sophisticated society or know the ins and outs of a successful **career** in the real world.

Are you sleep-deprived with a calendar full of **must-do** engagements? Pretend you are **jet-lagged**, and regale the crowds with stories of your latest cross-continental **romp**, as you struggle to keep your head from bobbing back while you lose **consciousness**. Chances are your tales of adventure will become even more interesting as you trail off to **sleep** mid-sentence.

Sending good **wishes** to all during the **holidays** is a welcome change from the nasty-spewing **evil-eyed** sentiments that are too often sent out during non-holiday times. **Auntie** knows you are just trying to be **polite**, but inserting that qualifying phrase, ***"to all those who celebrate,"*** is overly careful. Throw caution to the wind, and sincerely **heap** good cheer of all sorts on everyone. We all need as many good **thoughts** as possible these days.

Have you **encountered** a clerk or customer service rep with an **unnaturally** high, fake, sweet, little-girl voice? When asked, ***"How can I help you?"*** simply request that the **dear** clerk lower her voice by at least an **octave**. If this is not possible, start responding in kind—using your best squeaky-pitched **falsetto** until the call or encounter ends. This provides you with great **practice**, too; you never know when there will be a last-minute recasting of **Minnie** Mouse in an animated special.

Always have a short **acceptance** speech at the ready for those unexpected moments when you are **awarded** a seemingly out-of-the-blue **accolade** for your civic, artistic, or creative **endeavors**. You never know when a statuette will be thrust into your hands, with the **spotlight** on. Remember to be gracious, and when thanking all those who **helped** along the way, always take the high road, saving the inside **jokes** and **sniping** for another day.

Auntie could do without the term ***"bucket list."*** It is such a **silly** phrase; why not do all the fun, interesting things you'd like to do, and make it part of your everyday **life**? A true adventure is much more **mysterious** to the outside world when treated **modestly**, as an offhand, everyday **escapade**. I'd bet that HRH Elizabeth II doesn't have a bucket list. You don't need one, either. Perform your **deed**, and then regale us with your marvelous tale while sipping **Prosecco**.

Never let the **beige** brigade overpower your pizazz. **Remember**, any efforts to squelch your quirky point of view are just efforts to control from the scared **dullards** in your world. Be brave, and always be yourself—no doubt you'll end up **happier**, and most likely will **incorporate** the beige into your growing **entourage**.

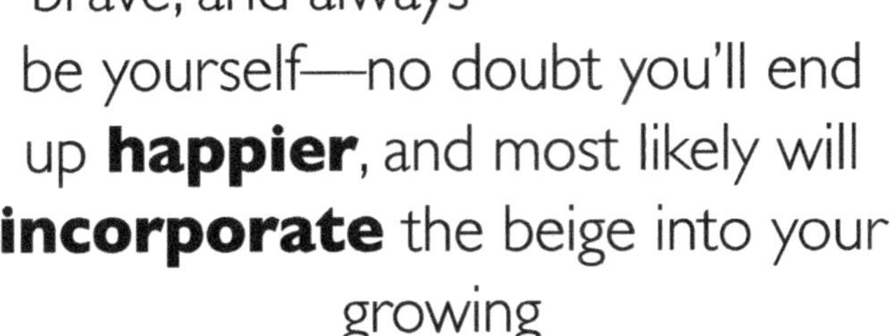

Auntie Jodi wants you to realize that your **public** and private group posts give us huge **clues** about your likes, dislikes, successes, failures, **kinks**, Achilles heels, and ever **so** much more. Do you really want all of us to know? We are more than able to connect the dots; **obviously**, your unconscious brain is unable to do so. Once read, these things are never unread. Perhaps a bit of **self-editing** might be in order.

Darlings, if you cannot speak on the telephone, do not pick up and tell the caller that, ***"I can't talk right now."*** This is what **caller I.D.** and **voicemail** are all about. Is there anything as **annoying** as having someone answer the phone, only to tell you that said person cannot answer the phone? If you have no time for a polite ***"Hello,"*** avoid all misunderstandings and hurt feelings by simply ignoring the call. This way, you avoid looking like a rude, **self-centered**, phone-addicted luddite.

Is that **pc-sanctioned** list of banned products, people, ideas, and programs growing by the **proverbial** leaps and bounds? Start your own list of The **Banned**. At the top of your list, place the people who compose those ridiculous **proscriptions**. One must refuse to be around the **ignorant**, the humorless, the controlling, and the unimaginative. Do not let them box you in—or out. Always be your fabulously **unique** self.

Sometimes **Auntie** feels for the **souls** of politicians, reporters, and yes, media **personalities**. It seems that despite the initial do-gooder/improve the world/ help **mankind** reasons for opting to go into these fields, more often than not, **egomania**/power/elitism takes the lead in the day-to-day lives of these dear ones—with the **ultimate** goal being to force their needs and desires upon us—the quaint and clueless ***"little folk."*** **Darlings**, a **polite** reminder—we are not quaint, and we certainly are not **clueless**.

You certainly **can** question authority; just **don't** doubt **Auntie** J.

1. What are some of your favorite items to drop in other shopper's carts?
2. When does Auntie suggest using hand sanitizer?
3. What's the difference between an insult and an anti-insult?

There's so much more online, sign up now and stay in contact with your Auntie, because you never call anymore.

auntiejodi.com

www.ingramcontent.com/pod-product-compliance
Lightning Source LLC
Chambersburg PA
CBHW070451120726
47910CB00003B/1001

9780990727606